There Is Magic
in the Blackberry Patch

S. YOLANDA ROBINSON M.Ed, AUTHOR
ILLUSTRATED BY KRISTI RANSOM STULTZ

This is a work of fiction. Incidents are a product of the author's imagination
or used fictitiously. Special thanks is given to the following individuals for
allowing us to use their name and images for this story:

Al Edmondson, A Cut Above the Rest

Khari Enaharo, Straight Talk Live

Eric Freeman

Allen Huff, Neighborhood House

Angela Pace, Chanel 10

All other characters and events written in the narrative and any
resemblance to them in this book living or dead is entirely coincidental.

****

Proceeds from this book will be given to support the children of Poindexter
Village in their college education and/or to start their own business.

This book was printed in the United States of America.

Rev. date: 02/06/2014

To order additional copies of this book, contact:
Xlibris Corporation
1-888-795-4274
www.Xlibris.com
Orders@Xlibris.com

ACKNOWLEDGEMENTS

First of all I would like to thank God for leading and guiding me to so many wonderful people while writing this book.

This book is historical children's fiction. It is written for the purpose of inspiring young children to get involved in their communities. Should they decide to do this, a whole new world will open up for them. Their academic studies will become more meaningful, they will have a lot of respect for the neighborhoods in which they live and most of all they will be prepared to help the next generation.

I did not do this alone. There was a lot of support given to me when I announced that I was writing a book on Poindexter Village and I am sincerely grateful to everyone who took the time to interview, share resources and be a listening ear through every step of the process of writing and publishing this book.

Most of my inspiration comes from Dr. Anna Bishop. Dr. Anna Bishop is the first person to write a book on Poindexter Village. Everyone who knew Dr. Bishop understands why you can't help but carry the torch that she gave to her students, friends, family, co-workers and pass it on.

I am grateful to the residents of Poindexter Village for sharing their stories, research and resources so that this book could be published.

Marilyn Cherry was one of those individuals who you could sit and talk to all about the Village for hours and not realize how much time it took. Also Barbara Lowry is another person. Barbara Lowry retired from Columbus Metropolitan Housing Authority (CMHA). Barbara shared with me the names of people who lived in Poindexter for our interviews.

Mike Cook knows everyone in Columbus, Ohio. There was not a week that went by that he would share a name or tell me about an event that happened.

Dr. Patricia Wingard Carson was a major motivating force behind this book. Dr. Carson edited the first version and provided advice and encouragement. Dr. Manzetta Jackson provided advice and was a listening ear.

Charles Tennant, Ella Coleman, Nikki Shearer Tilford, Nancie Ransom, Shawn Freeman, Adrienne Freeman, Reggie Anglen, Wanda White, Linda K. Jackson, Folami Binta Hunter, Laura Tompkins, Donna Latif, Barry Edney, Aaron Murphy, Henry Simpson and Sandra Jamison guided me to individuals and resources.

The videographers, Miles Curtiss and Alex McDougal Webber, are now part of my family. We have spent a lot of hours together interviewing people for the film documentary that they are producing on Poindexter Village. Both these men have unselfishly given their time to put this book and the documentary together.

Willis Brown, the president of The Historical Bronzeville Civic Association has also been supportive in every step of the process. The Historical Bronzeville Civic Association allowed me to work with them on the Poindexter Village History Festival that was sponsored in October, 2010. It was at this time that I facilitated the oral history workshop. This gave me an opportunity to talk to many individuals who lived in Poindexter.

The Columbus Housing Justice, A Cut above the Rest, The Neighborhood House and the Free Press, Talktainmentradio.com, Columbus Metropolitan Housing Authority and the Central Ohio United Way Partnership grant for their financial and in-kind support of this book.

I would also like to thank Kristi Stultz the illustrator of the book. Kristi is a truly talented young lady who puts a lot of love in everything she does.

The staff of Xlibris is first class. They treated my book in the same manner as if it were theirs. And I like that about them. I would recommend them to anyone who wants to self-publish.

Thanks to all my family for being a listening ear and supporting me. Rudolph Robinson, Wanda Phillips, Brenda Robinson, Tanya Reyes, Angela Robinson, Clay Robinson, Betty Harrison, Charlotte Ann Price and Ruthie Middlebrooks, Vanessa Harris, Charles Freeman, Victor Straughter and Debbie Gooch have encouraged me in many ways. Also supporting this project were my cousins Lucille Alexander, John Hardiman and James (Sonny) Robinson who died while I was doing the last part of the book.

There is a lot of history in Poindexter and in your own neighborhoods. I hope this book encourages the reader to find out more about the people who live in their community. Neighborhoods are more than buildings and flowers. They are people. People can either make them or break them.

PREFACE

There Is Magic In The Blackberry Patch is written for the sole purpose of inspiring children to become active participants in their own community. Although the story in the book is fictional, historical events and some of the individuals actually grew up in Poindexter Village. All have agreed to be a part of this story.

Approximately 50 people were interviewed for this book and the upcoming documentary, *The Poindexters,* that is directed by Miles Curtiss and Alex McDougall. Some of the interviews will be shared on the website.

Residents and people who knew them have many stories to share about Poindexter Village and the Blackberry Patch. There are many lessons that the reader can learn in every interview. There are themes of love, caring, respect, and survival. There are also themes of clean neighborhood and the village concept where the entire neighborhood contributed to the development of its children.

There was a period in history when neighbors were neighbors. I reflect on a similar experience in my own neighborhood while putting together this story. During that period neighborhoods were safe. And people genuinely cared about each other.

Writing this book gave me a stronger connection to the people who live in Poindexter Village. As I drive through Poindexter Village I reflect back on the work of individuals like The Reverend James Poindexter, Dr. Anna Bishop, Aminah Robinson, Oretha Edwards and many of the individuals who were interviewed for the upcoming documentary. And I silently thank God for their work.

It is my hope that the reader will share the same experience. Neighborhoods are more than buildings. They are comprised of people who either care or don't care. Love is powerful. It conquers everything. And it is healing. The love can start with you and extend itself throughout the community.

I extend my love to you and ask that you pass it on. God Bless You.

S. Yolanda Robinson

Chapter 1

CHAD AND JERROD

Chad and Jerrod were good friends. They were as close as Shrek and Donkey. Chad and Jerrod did everything together. They played basketball, football, and soccer and ate lunch. They even sat next to each other in school, that is, as much as their teacher would allow them.

Whenever you saw Chad, Jerrod was close by. He was either walking with Chad or running up behind him to catch up. They had a lot in common. Both of them loved to read comic books—especially the superhero comics (i.e., X-Men, Batman, Flash, Captain Marvel, Green Lantern, Superman, and Spiderman).

Jerrod had some rare comic books. He said rare comic books were worth a lot of money. He thought they were extremely interesting to read.

One Monday, after what seemed to be a long weekend before school, Chad told Jerrod that he had a dog named Bach. When Chad talked about Bach, he got very excited.

"Bach is the best dog in the whole wide world," Chad pronounced.

"Bach can do anything," he said. "He can stand up, sit down, shake your hand, roll over, fetch a ball, and bring it back to you. Having Bach around the house is like having Scooby-Doo or Snoopy," Chad told Jerrod.

One day after school, Jerrod decided he would sneak over Chad's house and see his dog Bach. When he told Chad what he intended to do, they both got together to make up their plan.

Jerrod planned to hurry home before his mom and dad arrived from work. Chad drew a map with the directions to his home on a piece of paper, and he put it in Jerrod's book bag.

They both timed Jerrod's visit so that he could be home before his parents arrived from work.

COTA, the local public bus, arrived at the bus stop near his home at 5:15 p.m. His mother and father did not arrive home until 6:00 p.m. This would give Jerrod enough time to get back home and they would never know that he stopped over Chad's house.

Chapter 2

JERROD MEETS BACH

On the following Tuesday, Jerrod put his plan to work. He sneaked on the school bus with Chad and hid under a blanket in the back of the bus.

When it was time for Chad to get off the bus, Jerrod hurried off as quickly as he could and hid behind the garbage can on the sidewalk in hopes that the bus monitor would not see him.

When Jerrod got off the bus, Chad stood up from behind the garbage can and watched it travel down the street until he could no longer see the bus. They both walked over to Chad's house.

Jerrod noticed that the houses in Chad's neighborhood were all the same. There were no flowers in his yard, and there was a lot of litter on the streets. Chad lived in a housing project called the Blackberry Patch.

Jerrod briefly thought of the difference in his neighborhood and Chad's. In his neighborhood, there was no litter on the ground and all the houses had rows of beautiful shrubbery and flowers.

Jerrod's bedroom was twice the size of Chad's tiny bedroom. Jerrod had a bedroom all to himself. His room had a computer, television, desk, and sofa. Chad had a single bed and bunk bed that he shared with his two brothers, Clay and Jacques.

Another difference between Chad and Jerrod was Chad had a cool dog named Bach. Jerrod did not have any pets.

Jerrod saw that everything Chad said about Bach was true. He admired Bach while he did everything Chad asked him to do.

"Stand up, Bach," Chad said. And Bach stood up. "Roll over," he commanded. Bach rolled over. Bach did many other commands.

After he was finished, Chad told Bach to shake Jerrod's hand; and Bach went over to Jerrod, lifted his paw, and shook his hand. It seemed as though Bach was enjoying showing Jerrod what he could do as much as Jerrod enjoyed watching him. It is true, Jerrod thought, Bach is just as smart as Snoopy, Scooby-Doo, or any Disney dog.

Jerrod immediately fell in love with Bach. He wanted to have a dog like Bach so that he and Chad could have something else to share together. Jerrod could not wait to get home to ask his mother and father for a dog like Bach.

After Jerrod met Bach, he got on the COTA bus and waved goodbye to Chad. While riding home, Jerrod kept thinking about Bach. The pleasant thoughts Jerrod had about Bach shifted to fear as he walked home from the bus stop. Jerrod knew he was in trouble when he looked at the front yard of his home. There were police cars parked in the driveway and people standing in the yard talking to his mom and dad.

Chapter 3

JERROD ARRIVES HOME

When Jerrod's mother saw him, she had tears in her eyes. She looked at him and said, "Jerrod! Where have you been? We have been looking all over the neighborhood and school for you."

Jerrod shamefully put his head down and softly said, "I went over to Chad's house. I wanted to see his new dog named Bach."

His mother said, "Who is Chad?"

"I have never met him," said his dad.

"Where does he live?" Jerrod's mother asked.

Jerrod answered in a softer voice, "The Blackberry Patch."

"What did you say?" said Jerrod's mother.

"The Blackberry Patch," Jerrod answered.

Everyone said, "The Blackberry Patch!"

"Listen, young man," said Jerrod's mother, "I do not ever want you to go there again! And stay away from that Chad fellow. Nothing good has ever come out of that neighborhood!"

Jerrod had mixed feelings. He loved his mother and father. He also loved Chad. How could they say that nothing good has ever come out of that neighborhood? Chad was not a bad person. He is my best friend, he thought. Jerrod liked Chad's brothers, Jacques and Clay. It seemed as though everything about Chad was cool.

He could not understand what his mother and father meant when they said that nothing good ever came out of Chad's neighborhood.

Chapter 4

JERROD AND CHAD ARE NOT FRIENDS

The next day at school things were not the same. Jerrod kept his distance from Chad. Every time Chad tried to say something or talk to him, Jerrod had short answers, avoiding long conversations.

He made up many excuses on why he could not be with him at recess to play basketball and read comic books. Everyone at school noticed Jerrod was acting strange. Even the teacher noticed and said, "Are you all right, Jerrod?"

"Yeah, man, are you all right? Something must be wrong. You act as though I did not brush my teeth or take a bath this morning. And you know my mother would not let any of us leave the house dirty," Chad said.

"There is nothing wrong," Jerrod replied. But Jerrod's behavior continued to be strange all week. He waited until Friday when school ended to tell Chad the truth about what was really going on with him.

As Chad was getting on the bus, Jerrod said to him with a stuttering voice, "My, my, my mother and father told me to stay away from you because nothing good has ever come out of the Blackberry Patch."

"What?" Chad said.

"We cannot be friends because my mother and father said nothing good has ever come out of the Blackberry Patch," Jerrod said again.

All of a sudden a warm breeze came over Chad. His face felt like it was on fire. And his stomach got warm. Even though other children were talking and playing around, Jerrod's words kept spinning around in his head echoing the phrases "Nothing good has ever come out of the Blackberry Patch. Nothing good has ever come out of the Blackberry Patch . . ." These words repeated over and over in his mind.

Getting off the bus, Chad noticed many things that he had not seen before. He saw the litter on the ground and the houses with no flowers in front of them.

Jerrod's mother and father are right, he thought. How could any good come out of this? All this paper and broken glass on the streets—nothing good can come from this!

I wish I could run away and never come back here again, he thought to himself.

Chad went home and fed Bach. And then he went over to the recreation center to play basketball and work out his frustrations. Mr. Davis, the director of the center, noticed

Chad was acting strange. But he decided to leave him alone. Chad felt real bad. The pain would not go away. He lost his best friend because of the Blackberry Patch.

I hate this place, he thought. No one cares about the Blackberry Patch. No one picks up paper and the broken glass.

On Monday, Chad reluctantly woke up for school. He did not want to go to school and see Jerrod.Seeing Jerrod would remind him of what he said about the Blackberry Patch. He tried to act as though he was sick, but his mother made him go to school anyway.

Every time someone looked at Chad and smiled, he thought they were secretly laughing at him because he lived in the Blackberry Patch.

A few weeks later, the school had a big assembly for black history month. Chad did not know that this was a very important day in his life.

Chapter 5

THE BIG ASSEMBLY

At the assembly, Angela Pace, the local news anchor for Channel 10 and Khari Enaharo, the radio host of Straight Talk Live, spoke. They both gave inspirational speeches. They talked about the importance of making good grades, never giving up, and having a positive attitude.

All of the students in the school thought Angela Pace was tight. They also liked Khari. Chad remembered his mom and dad talking about Straight Talk Live. His dad would often become frustrated because he could never get on the air to express his opinions. The telephone lines were always busy.

Khari Enaharo and Angela Pace's words did not mean anything to Chad until after he heard the discussion they had with a group of students who gathered around them after their speech to ask questions.

Angela Pace asked students in the group what they wanted to be when they grew up. Salena said an actress. William wanted to be an artist. Mirah said a radio host. Jerrod said a doctor. Angela looked at Chad, and he put his head down and said nothing.

Jerrod told Angela that Chad lived in the Blackberry Patch and nothing good ever comes from the Blackberry Patch. Chad started to run away from the group but stopped when Angela said something that surprised everyone.

"I grew up in the Blackberry Patch," she said. "When I was there it was called Poindexter Village. It has a lot of history. Many famous people grew up there.

"Yes, did you know that the Blackberry Patch has magic in it?"

"Magic?" said all the boys and girls.

"Yes, if you do good things to the Blackberry Patch, good things will happen to you," Angela said.

"The famous artist Aminah Robinson painted historical pictures of the Blackberry Patch and Poindexter Village. And today her work is shown all over the world."

"I think I saw her painting last year when we went on a field trip. Does she have her painting displayed in the Freedom Museum in Cincinnati, Ohio?" Mirah asked.

"Yes," said Khari. "Mr. Poindexter started making positive changes in the neighborhood, and he became the first African American elected to city council. At one time the Blackberry Patch was named Poindexter Village after Mr. Poindexter.

"Dr. Anna Bishop wrote many stories about the Blackberry Patch. Her picture is on the wall of the King Arts Complex.

"When I lived in Poindexter Village, there were so many people who inspired me,"

Angela said.

Chad's face lit up, and the burning inside changed from hot to warm when he heard Angela Pace ask Jerrod, "I grew up in the Blackberry Patch. Do you think that I am no good?"

"No way," he said. And the rest of the boys and girls said, "We think you are cool."

Angela Pace continued talking to students about the people who grew up in Poindexter Village (also known as the Blackberry Patch).

"The Blackberry Patch has doctors, lawyers, artists, firemen, teachers, nurses, beauticians, computer scientists, preachers, policemen, business owners, ministers, and many other professionals," Angela pronounced.

"If it was so great, why did you leave?" William asked.

"No one ever leaves the Patch," Angela said.

"Just like Aminah Robinson's famous paintings and Dr. Bishop's book about the Blackberry Patch, its memories will always be with us. It was where we all started," she said.

Chapter 6

BACK IN THE DAY

That day after school, Chad got off the bus, and something magical happened. The Blackberry Patch felt different. Even though it had litter on the streets, Chad could feel a change was coming.

When Chad's mother took him to get his hair cut at A Cut Above the Rest barbershop, he told Mr. Al about Angela Pace's speech.

Chad was surprised to learn that Mr. Al grew up across the street from the Blackberry Patch. When Mr. Al announced that he grew up there, he gave the entire shop a history about the Blackberry Patch and Poindexter Village. He started most of his sentences with "back in the day" with excitement in his voice.

"Back in the day, the Blackberry Patch had parades," he said. "There were many businesses near the Patch back in the day. Famous people and groups visited the Patch.

People like Presidents Roosevelt and Carter and Motown entertainers like the Temptations and the Impressions."

"Back in the day, the Blackberry Patch had one of the largest African American festivals in the United States," one of the customers in the shop said.

"We all did the electric slide on the street, and we broke the Guinness Book of Records. We had twenty thousand people on the street doing the electric slide. Mayor Michael Coleman led the electric slide line," Mr. Al said.

"Back in the day, we had good food and jazz in the Blackberry Patch," Mr. Al said.

Another customer said, "Everyone went to the Marble Gang."

"The Marble Gang?" somebody said. "What about the 502 Club, the Macon and Sandy's, and the Jamaica Club? Did you know the original owner of the Marble Gang started Glory Food? His name is Bill Williams."

"It seems as though everyone in Poindexter Village attended Union Grove Baptist Vacation Bible School in the summers.

The younger children were either in Ohio Day Care or CMACAO Head Start." said another customer.

"Yes I remember back in the day when Lolita Clark was a teacher and later became the director of CMACAO Head Start.

She grew up right across the street from the village," Mr. Al replied.

Mr. Al got so excited he clipped Chad's ear

"Ouch!" Chad screamed out loud.

Back in the day, the Patch was called Poindexter Village.

"Do you remember when Poindexter Village had the large carnival during the summer?" said one of the customers.

"I remember the annual tennis match that was organized by the staff at Beatty Park.

Now that was a sight to see. Everyone would dress up just to watch people play tennis. And people from all over the city came." Another customer said.

"And back in the day, we had good teachers. I had Mr. Ed Willis. He was like a father to me. He expected us to do well in school. My mother would allow him to discipline me if I acted up in school," said Ann as she was getting her hair put into tiny curls.

"Back in the day, Poindexter Village had the prettiest lawns in the city. Mr. Colwell and the residents did not allow any trash on their lawn," said another customer. "If you threw trash on the lawn, someone would either pick it up or ask you to pick it up."

"Even though we were poor, we never thought about it. We had everything because the people in Poindexter cared about each other. I could leave my door open and no one would come in and rob me. If we had little food, we would put it together and make one big meal," he continued.

"What happened?" said Chad. "When they took away the name Poindexter, the history got lost," said another customer. "The Blackberry Patch is its original name, and then it was named Poindexter Village after Mr. James Poindexter. Mr. Poindexter meant a lot to our city—particularly to African Americans. He was a minister, business owner, and the first African American to be elected to an office in our city. Poindexter Village was the first government housing project in the United States. When a private owner purchased Poindexter Village, he changed the name back to the Blackberry Patch," said an older customer.

"When we lost the history, the neighborhood pride was lost also," said another customer.

"Angela Pace said if you are good to the Blackberry Patch, it will be good to you.

Is it true?" Chad asked Mr. Al.

"That's what everyone says about the Blackberry Patch. Well, son, I guess you never know unless you try," Mr. Al replied.

Chapter 7

THE MAGIC BEGINS

Walking home after his haircut, Chad thought about what Mr. Al and Angela Pace said. He thought about the history of the Blackberry Patch. Is it true? Is there really magic in the Blackberry Patch? What is the magic? he thought. Well, I guess I am going to have to find out when I do something good for the Blackberry Patch, he thought.

The conversation with Chad got Mr. Al thinking. Talking about the good times he had in the Blackberry Patch made him and his customers happy. The next day Mr. Al brought his back-in-the-day pictures and hung them on the wall of his barbershop.

Word got around town about Mr. Al's back-in-the-day pictures. People from all over the city came to see them and talk about their experience in the Patch as they got their hair cut.

Angela Pace did a television special highlighting Mr. Al's back-in-the-day pictures. Mr. Al's business grew after that. In fact it got so large that he had to add some more rooms to his shop.

Chad started picking up trash in the Patch right after he left the barbershop. As he was picking up trash, he saw a man picking up the trash and putting it into a beautiful case.

"What are you going to do with that trash?" Chad asked. "This is my material for the art that I do. I make sculptures, vases, hanging wall pictures, and whatever the spirit leads me to make with these pieces. This trash is someone else's treasures," said Eric Freeman. "There is no way you can make something out of these bent cans," Chad said. "If you give me your cans and bottles, I will show you what I am doing. My shop is right over there." And he pointed to his house. "Stop over and I will show you. But you must first ask your mother and father if it is okay," said Mr. Freeman. Chad immediately gave him all the cans and bottles he collected in the Patch.

When he went home, he asked his mother if he could go over to Eric Freeman's house.

His mother said she would go with him. And she did. When they arrived over to Eric Freeman's home, they saw a lot of sculptures and wall hangings on the porch. They are beautiful. "I wish I could do that," said Chad. "I will teach you, if it is okay with your mother," said Eric. And his mother gave him permission to work with Eric Freeman. For several weeks Chad went over to Eric's house where he showed him how to sterilize the trash and shape it into a piece of art.

Mr. Eric also told Chad stories about back in the day. He said when the children of Poindexter Village grew up, they did some wonderful things for the community. "There is a movie called Fight for Life starring Morgan Freeman and Jerry Lewis that talks about how Dr. Earl Sherard helped save a little girl's life that had epilepsy. And later he was the director of the epilepsy clinic at Children's Hospital which is now called Nationwide Children's Hospital.

Dr. Sherard lived in Poindexter Village. Myron Lowery became the mayor of Memphis, Tennessee. John Foster started an engineering business and hired many of the kids who grew up with him. Yes, Chad, when people lost the history, people forgot. If someone tells you that nothing good has ever came from the Blackberry Patch, they do not know the history of the Patch. You have to ask someone my age, they know," he said.

After leaving his art lesson with Mr. Freeman, Chad got an idea. He wanted to surprise his mother and give her one of the beautiful flower pots for her porch. He also asked his mother if she would give him some money to plant some flowers. And she did. Chad put the soil into each pot and planted the flowers. Each day he watered them. The flowers and vases were so beautiful that their neighbors wanted their yard to look like Chad's. His next-door neighbor said they would pay Chad to do their porch. Each time he did a porch, someone in the next house would ask him how much he would charge to do theirs. And before you knew it, there was an entire section of the Patch that had porches with beautiful flowers.

As you walked through the Blackberry Patch, it started to look like it had been described as back in the day. There was no trash on the street, and the yards looked beautiful—

particularly with the new flowers and flower pots on the porch. The entire neighborhood started picking up trash and saving it so that they could get Chad to make flower pots for their porch.

Each time Chad made money, he put some in church and saved some. And Chad's business increased.

The Blackberry Patch began to look beautiful. People who lived in the Blackberry Patch appeared to be happier. As Chad worked on the yards in his neighborhood, other children asked if they could help him. Chad paid them part of what he made.

While doing the lawn, Chad thought about the history lessons he learned. Yes, the

Blackberry Patch deserves to be beautiful, he said to himself as he put flowers in the vases. And it is beautiful. The flower pots, flowers, and other decorations with recycled materials gave the Blackberry Patch that added touch that was unique and beautiful.

Word began to spread around city about the Blackberry Patch's new look. People from all over the city came to see the yards.

When Mr. Allen Huff from the Neighborhood House heard about what Chad did for the Blackberry Patch, he invited him to join the Neighborhood House's Young Entrepreneurs' Association. The Neighborhood House is an organization that has a lot of respect in the Blackberry Patch. It has helped many families in the city. Chad was happy that Mr. Huff wanted him to be a member of their association.

Chad started going to meetings. The meetings were very interesting. It helped him with his business. He learned about profit and loss and marketing strategies. It also helped Chad with his math. After attending several meetings, Chad's math scores went from 70s to 90s and 100s. His business also increased so much that Chad had people ordering his vases from all over the city. A lot of people liked the idea that he was recycling trash.

Chapter 8

BACH STEALS THE SHOW

One day when Chad came from school, there was an envelope addressed to his mom that said, "To the parents of Chad Harrison." It was from the mayor's office.

When Mrs. Harrison opened the envelope and pulled out the letter, she read it.

It said that Chad was selected to receive the Community Pride Award at the Poindexter Village History Festival. The ceremony will be held on October 9 on the grounds of the Beatty Park Recreation Center.

Chad was so excited. He could not imagine being selected for the award. And he started counting the days when the ceremony would begin.

On Saturday, October 9, Chad got up and looked out his window. It was a beautiful day. The sun was bright and the Blackberry Patch looked beautiful. It appeared as though everyone was happy. As he, his mom, and his brothers walked up to the Beatty Park Recreation Center, they could hear beautiful music outside. People were greeting each other with hugs and smiles like they had not seen each other in a long time. These people were the residents and the former residents of Poindexter Village. They came from all around the country to participate in the Poindexter Village History Festival. All of them were happy about how the way Blackberry Patch looked. Some of them said it reminded them of back in the day when they lived in Poindexter Village.

Bach came to the ceremony with Chad. Both of them went on the stage for the award when Mayor Coleman called Chad's name. The only problem was Bach. When Chad walked on the stage with Bach, Bach took a bow and put his paw out to shake the mayor's hand. The audience forgot Chad was being honored. They cheered for Bach and asked him to do it again. And Bach did. Bach loved it.

Jerrod was in the audience with his mom and dad. Jerrod's father also received an award for his outstanding contributions in the community.

Jerrod said, "Look Mom there's my friend Chad. He is with Bach. I miss them. I told you Bach is as smart as Scooby-Doo or Snoopy."

He certainly is an intelligent young man. I believe he is going to do more great things for this community and our city. I never knew all these people grew up here. I have worked with many of them. Sybil McNabb is the state president of the NAACP. I remember her sister, Sharlene Morgan, when she was president of the school board. Your dad has some of Steve Paco's music at home, and Gwen Rodgers sold us our house."

Jerrod's mother took his dad's hand and said, "Let's go over and meet Chad's mom."

As they walked over, Jerrod asked his father, "Can I have a dog like Bach? Can I? I would love to have a dog like Bach."

"Me too, but we have to talk about that later," Jerrod's dad said.

After the ceremony when they all arrived home, Chad reminded his mom about what Angela Pace and Mr. Al said.

"It's true," Chad said. "What everyone said about the Patch is true."

"What on earth are you talking about? What is true?" asked Mrs. Harrison.

"Good things happen to me when I did good things for the Blackberry Patch," Chad said, as he placed his award on the television in the living room.

"Yes, Chad, the magic is the love. Magic happens when you put love in your community. And that's what happened to you. It not only happened to you, it happened for the entire community. Everyone benefits. No one loses. You have made all of us very proud of you," Mrs. Harrison said.

Chad smiled and put his award on top of the television.

APPENDICES

APPENDIX I   ACADEMIC CONTENT STANDARDS & LESSON PLANS

1. Social Studies programs should provide a study of culture. **Social Science**

2. Social Studies programs should include an experience that provides for individual development and identity. Social Studies program should demonstrate pride in personal accomplishments and obtain information about a topic using a variety of oral and visual resources. *Social Science*

3. Students will demonstrate active listening strategies (asking focused questions, responding to cues, making visual contacts). *Language Arts*

4. Students will deliver informational presentations (e.g., expository research) that:

    a. Demonstrate an understanding of the topic and present events and ideas in a logical sense *Language Arts*

    b. Support the main idea with relevant facts, details, examples, quotations, statistics, Stories and anecdotes; *Language Arts*

    c. Organize information, including a clear introduction, body and conclusion and follow common organizational structures when appropriate (eg., cause-effect, compare-contrast). *Language Arts*

LESSON PLANS

Lesson Summary

Students will learn about the neighborhood history through oral interviews and research in the library.

Estimated Duration: 40 hours broken into short sessions.

Instructional Procedures

1. Students write questions that they want to know about their neighborhood.

2. Students spend time at the library reviewing historical events in their neighborhood.

3. Students prepare a chronological list of historical events.

4. Students have an open discussion indicating some of the questions that they will ask.

5. Students add or delete to the questions they will be asking.

Homework Option and Home Connections

1. Students interview business, neighbors and family members who live in their neighborhood.

2. Students should collect and take pictures comparing what the neighborhood is now and what it was like in the past.

3. Prepare the presentation on the computer.

4. Prepare a series of questions regarding the neighborhood (ask about community leaders, accomplishments, historical events)

5. Interview neighbors using cell phones or cameras. Prepare a presentation on the computer.

6. Organize a neighborhood clean up drive, garage sale and/or work with the neighborhood civic association.

7. Work on a community garden and/or volunteer to work at the recreation center/and or church

8. Begin a campaign to help homeless, veterans, and sick people. Visit nursing homes.

9. What did you learn from the experience?

Materials Needed

Computers, cell phones, cameras, paper and pencil

Pre Test

1. What do you know about your neighborhood?

2. Who are the community leaders?

3. What did they do to make things better?

4. What businesses contribute to the neighborhood?

5. How do they contribute?

6. What programs do they have at the recreation centers?

7. What does the neighborhood do for children?

8. Is your neighborhood safe?

9. Does your neighborhood have a civic association and/or block watch?

10. What are the future plans for your neighborhood?

APPENDIX II   WHAT HAPPENED TO THE PEOPLE WHO LIVED IN POINDEXTER VILLAGE

Mozelle Allen*	Center Manager, Head Start
James Austin	CEO, Creative Software
Carla Pace Banner	Insurance Agent
Hugh Black	North American Rockwell
David Black	Teacher, Columbus City Schools
James Black	State Worker D.C
James Blackenberry	Plumber
Richard Blackenberry	Manger, Isabelle Ridgeway Nursing Home
Charlene Bonderount	Housewife and retired from Schottenstein store
George Boston	Dentists, Associate Professor, The Ohio State University
	first African American to receive tenure at OSU
Robert Brown	President, Columbus Urban League
Rodger Brown	Retired from Juvenile Delinquent Center
James Brown	Singer for Four Mints
Rusty Bryant	Musician and recording artist
Howard Burks*	School Teacher, Columbus City Schools
Charles Comer	Football Coach, Western Michigan University
Douglas Comer	Author, Columbus Parks and Recreation
Lucille Cherry	Electronics, North American Aviation
Marilyn Kendrick Cherry*	Administrative Clerk, John E. Foster and Associates Purchasing Agent, USA Skates
Bernard Cherry	Manager, Ben Cramer & Son Paint Store Manager, Poindexter Village

Sam Cherry	Air Craft Spray Painter, McDonald Douglas
Lynn Stowe Cousar	State Worker, State of Ohio
Barbara Cunningham	President, Poindexter Resident Council
James Howard Dawson	Maintenance Technician, The Ohio State University
Ike Day	Art Teacher
Robin Pace DeLoach	Works for a nursing home
Betty Drummond	Columbus School Board Member
Grady Doughty	Minister
Shelly Doughty	Worked with the Rev. Jesse Jackson and the Rainbow Coalition
Marcelyn Keys Dyer	Secretary, St. Phillips Lutheran Church
Oretha Edwards*	Chair, Poindexter History Festival
Reginald Edwards	Electrical Engineer, ATT, Minister Christ Memorial
Sybil Edwards McNabb*	State President, NAACP, owner, McNabbs Funeral Home
John E. Foster	Author, owner, John E. Foster & Associates, civil sanitary and Architectural and survey company, engineer for the vocal point in Mt. Vernon plaza
Newton Foster	Civil Engineer, Deputy Director, Technical Operations Wright Patterson Air Force Base
Adrienne Freeman	School Teacher, Columbus City Schools
Samuel J. Freeman, Sr.	Neil House Hotel And Vice President of Local Union of Lennox Industries
Samuel Freeman, Jr.	retired General Motors
Leroy Galloway	Owner of Gally's restaurant
Billy Graham	aka Wild Bill Graham Owner of Escalators
Cecil Granger	Stock Handler, General Motors
Kathleen Gravely	Stay at Home Mom

Steve Paco Grier*	Musician, recording artist and Social Activist
Alice Carol Grant	Dance Instructor, Danced with Pearl Bailey Dancers
Barbara Blackwell Harris	Dance Instructor
Diane Hawkins	Operative Technician, Children's Hospital
Charles Haynes, Sr.	Fork lift Operator, Department of Defense
Charles Haynes, Jr.	Buyer, Shoe Corporation
Shirley Haynes	Cashier, Big Bear
Van Haynes	Counselor, Youth Services
Shermaine Stowe Hill	Defense Construction Supply Company
Donald Hinton	St. Stephens Recreation Center
Larry Hinton	U.S. Post Office
Lorena Hinton	Cosmetologist
Folami Binta Hunter*	(aka Pat Ware) CEO, 2 B Natural By Design

Steve and Terry Jackson Family 1980-1994

Steven Jackson	Correction Officer, Ohio Department of Correction
Terry Jackson	Account
Shante Jackson	Loan Officer, Chase Bank
Stephanie Jackson	Co Manager, Shoe Who
Ton-ya Jackson	Manager, Eistine Bagos
Charles James	YMCA, Ohio Civil Rights Commission
Allen Johnson	Pulmonary Technician
Luther Johnson	Defense Construction Supply Center, Supervisor
August Jones	Housekeeper, Upper Arlington
Beverly Jones	Military widow
Richard Jones	St. Stephens Recreation Center
Sundiata Kata	Director, Sundiata Kata Music School

aka Francis Irving	San Diego, California
Charles Keaton*	City of Columbus
Dorothy Keaton*	Cashier, Rosetta Store and Defense Construction Supply Company
Jean Robinson Christian Keller	Keller House, Portland, Oregon
	owned 7 Group Homes for children and adults in Portland, Oregon
Barbara Kendrick	Supply clerk, Defense Construction Supply Co.
William Kendrick (1940s)	Custodian, Poindexter Village, Beatty Park Recreation Center
Richard Keyes	Instructor, Fresno State College and Entrepreneur
Roy Keyes	Postal Worker
Josephine Pride Mac	Organist and Union Grove
Norma Jean Jones McCall	Defense Construction Supply Center
Carol Jones Pace Dulaney	Defense Construction Supply Center
Bo Lamar	NBA Basketball player, Played with Detroit Pistons, Los Angeles Lakers, San Diego Sails, San Diego Conquistadors Indiana Pacers
Lawrence Laws	Entrepreneur
Myron Lowery	Former interim mayor & President of City Council, Memphis, Tennessee
Carolyn Martin	State Worker
Robert Martin	Navy, retired Baxton Health Care
Barbara McCarroll	School Teacher, Columbus City Schools
Jay Mitchell	Cement Mason
Donna Mitchell	Cashier, Rosettes, receptionist Children's Hospital
Sofia Mohammed	Graduated with honors, enrolled at The Ohio State University

Fred Modena*	North American Rockwell
Marilyn Robinson Montgomery	General Motors
Saundra Montgomery	State Worker
Sue Montgomery	General Motors
Charlene Morgan	School Board President
Grace Edwards Mullins	Owner, Barber Shop and local activist for Mt. Vernon Avenue Organizer of Comin Home Festival
Vivian Mullins	Royal Barbeque (worker in her father's family owned business)
Alfreda Barbour Nichols	LPN, worked for General Motors
Chief Shongo Obadina	Executive Director and Curator, William H. Thomas Gallery
Angela Pace*	News Anchor and Director of Community Affairs, WBNS-TV
Norma Pearson	Homemaker
Donald Robinson	Graduated from Oakwood College
Gwen Robinson	Receptionist
Richard Robinson	Retired, Air Force
Terrill Patrick Taylor	Marketing Director for John Fosters, Inc.
Barbara Kendrick Pattrick 1940-1952	Defense Construction Supply Center
Joseph Pride 1940	Minister in Virginia
Lewis Pryor	Forman, Machine Shop, North American Aviation
June Neff Rasberry 1950	Retired from Defense Construction Supply Center
Aminah (Brenda) Robinson	Artist, McArthur Fellow
Carolyn Coulson Roddy	Stay at home mom, married Pastor Earnest Roddy
Gwendolyn Rogers	Real Estate Agent, Teacher, and Community Advocate
Jimmy Rodgers	Musician, played with Hank Mawr, Rusty Bryant and Sammy Davis

Paul Shearer	Social Services, Supervisor, Atlanta, Georgia
William Shearer*	Owner, KGFJ, Radio in Los Angeles, California
Earl Sherard, M. D.	Medical Doctor, Morgan Freeman played him in the Movie Fight for Life. He brought to Europe and brought a cure back to the United States for Epilepsy.
Allen Stowe	Clerk, Advertising Checking Bureau
Rodger Stowe	Director, Minority Affairs, State of Ohio Treasurer's Office
Julie Whitney Scott	Author, Radio Host for talktainmentradio.com
Evelyn Kendrick Smith 1940-1950	Head Start Center Manager
Cecil Smith	General Motors
Reita Smith	Health Coach, local historian, community advocate
Karen Keyes Taylor	wife of Charles Taylor, former President of Wilberforce University
Bill Thornton	Owner, Toast of the Town

The Tidwells moved to Poindexter Village in 1940 and left in 1950

Eugene Tidwell	North American Rockwell
Viola Tidwell	House Wife and Stay at Home Mom
Carl Tidwell	General Motors
Donald Tidwell	General Motors, owner Construction Company and Golden Bird Chicken
Howard Tidwell	General Motors
Kenny Tidwell	State Farm Agent
Rodger Tidwell	General Motors
Nikki Shearer Tilford	Graduated from Central State University with a major in English, Author, wrote in Chicken Soup, African American Soul, Chicken Soup for African American Women, and is currently writing the history on Isabelle Ridgeway

Barbara Tolbert*	Secretary, Columbus City Schools Executive Board Member;
Helen Tolbert	Parks and Recreation, Charlotte, North Carolina
James Tolbert	Lennox Factory
John Tolbert	Counselor, City of Columbus, Alcohol Anonymous
Jordan Tolbert	Universal Studio, California
Thelma Kendrick Truss	License Practical Nurse
Clifford Tyree	Founder, I Know I Can, community advocate for children
Howard Tyler	Insurance Agent

The Tuney Family Moved to Poindexter in 1940s

Ann Tuney	Western Electric
Dorothy Tuney	Nurse
Etta Tuney	Cook at Champion, Jr. High
Hubert Tuney	Tuney's Carry Out, Airport Sky Cap and owner of Golden Bird Chicken
Wilford Tuney, Sr.	City of Columbus and owner of Golden Bird Chicken,

The Ollie Mae & Emmett Walker Family 1953-1968

Albert Walker	Bank Manager
Anna Walker	Dialysis Technician
Charles Walker	Supervisor, The Ohio State University
Jerry Walker*	Special Needs Teacher
Larry Walker	Teacher, Basketball Coach, East High School
Ollie Mae Walker	Supervisor Jefferson Hotel
Robert Walker	Manager, Safety & Crime Prevention
Shirley Walker	Secretary

William Walker	Buyer, Sears, Chicago, Illinois and a Police Officer
Bertha Washington (1940)	
Clara Washington	Defense Construction Supply Center
Elizabeth Washington	Defense Construction Supply Center
Harvey Washington	Minister
Ethel White	Domestic Worker
Gaynell Wicks	Owner, Day Care Business
Elizabeth (Crystal) Stowe Windham	Attended Allen University

*Interviewed for film documentary on Poindexter as of 8/11/2011

Also interviewed are the following businesses:

1. A Cut Above the Rest

2. Crawley's Frame

3. Mayo's Printing

4. Stewarts Memorial

APPENDIX III   POINDEXTER VILLAGE
HISTORICAL EVENTS

1940   the first public housing project in Columbus was opened by President Franklin D. Roosevelt. It is called Poindexter Village.

1940   February 18, 1940 Aminiah Robinson was born. It was the same day her family moved to Poindexter Village. Aminiah Robinson is an artist who has historical paintings of Poindexter Village and the near eastside of Columbus displayed around the world. The areas once known as the Blackberry Patch, was primarily farm land located on the edge of Columbus, Ohio.

1975   Poindexter Village Reunion, held in the Poindexter Village Administration Building

1982   *Beyond the Blackberry Patch* authored by Dr. Anna Bishop, The Public Library of Columbus and Franklin County

1983   *A Fight for Life* was released. This is a movie on Dr. Earl Sherard who lived in Poindexter Village. Morgan Freeman plays Dr. Sherard.

1990   April 20, 1990 Today show was aired on the site of Poindexter Village for Earth Day,

1997   *A Street Called Home*, authored by Aminiah Robinson, Harcourt Brace & Company.

2010   October 2, 2010 Poindexter History Festival was held at Beatty Park Recreation Center

2011   April 21, 2011 WOSU Airs a documentary on the Bronzeville King-Lincoln District that includes the Blackberry Patch (Poindexter Village)

2011   *There Is Magic in The Blackberry Patch* authored by S. Yolanda Robinson, Xlibris.

2011   The Poindexters (a film documentary produced by Miles Curtiss and Alex McDougal Webber)

2012   *Beyond the Blackberry Patch* will be shown at the King Lincoln Theater

APPENDIX IV PICTURES

The Blackberry Patch in the 1930s

Poindexter Village in the 1940s

Poindexter Village 2011

S. YOLANDA ROBINSON was raised on the east side of Columbus, Ohio. She is an East High School graduate. Yolanda received her master's degree in education from the University of Massachusetts at Amherst.

Yolanda has a passion for working with children and families. Each week she hosts a live internet program produced by Talktainmentradio called "All in Our Family." She said, "It's for the sole purpose of strengthening families." Yolanda has worked as an administrator and tutor for an afterschool tutoring program, as a reading instructional coach, and as a job-readiness program instructor. In her own family she annually publishes a family newsletter, hosts family events, such as family reunions, and often has family prayer in her home. Yolanda is a peer reviewer for the Corporation of National and Community Services. She is a member of Trinity Baptist Church in Columbus, Ohio.

In her career, Yolanda has received many honors. She is a recipient of an Ohio State University (OSU) Affirmative Action award, OSU Women Coming Together Advocate of the Year award, and Avery International award. She was nominated for the Carter G. Woodsen Award by the United States Department of Defense for her work with children and families. The department which she managed for CMACAO (Columbus Metropolitan Area Community Action Organization) Head Start was the recipient of the John Glenn Best Practice award for its work with low income families.

Yolanda has chaired numerous committees. She was one of the ground level organizers of the Family and Medical Leave Act (FMLA). She was the president of Cardinal Chapter of Nine to Five. She was interviewed on the "Today Show" for her participation. As president, Yolanda served on the African American Triumphs Consortium. Yolanda was a national conference chair for the National Council for Black Studies. She was also Secretary of the Ohio Black Studies Consortium.

Although still very active, Yolanda has retired from her job as the acting program manager for the OSU Black Studies Extension Center. Her membership involvement includes the Coalition of 100 Black Women in Columbus. As the mother of Chad Heath Robinson, Yolanda is the grandmother of Akeisheunte and Yazmina.

Yolanda said "This book is written to inspire children to get involved in their communities. Proceeds from the book will go toward helping the children who live in Poindexter Village receive scholarship and or support to start their own business. If the book does this, it will accomplish its goal."

CPSIA information can be obtained at www.ICGtesting.com
Printed in the USA
LVIW01n1430270618
582071LV00003B/20